Omar On Board

Maryann Kovalski

Fitzhenry & Whiteside

For Gregory

Copyright © 2005 by Maryann Kovalski

Published in Canada by Fitzhenry & Whiteside,
195 Allstate Parkway, Markham, Ontario L3R 4T8

Published in the United States by Fitzhenry & Whiteside,
121 Harvard Avenue, Suite 2, Allston, Massachusetts 02134

10 9 8 7 6 5 4 3 2 1

Library and Archives Canada Cataloguing in Publication

Kovalski, Maryann
Omar on board / Maryann Kovalski.

ISBN 1-55041-918-8

I. Title.

PS8571.O96O49 2005   jC813'.54   C2004-906853-9

**U.S. Publisher Cataloging-in-Publication Data
(Library of Congress Standards)**

Kovalski, Maryann.
Omar on Board / Maryann Kovalski
[32] p.: col. ill.; cm.
Summary: Omar isn't nearly as good as his friends at
swimming or jumping off the high-diving board
but when it comes to helping a friend, Omar forgets all about his fears.

ISBN 1-55041-918-8

1. Friendship – Fiction. I. Title.
[E] 22   PZ7.K68Om 2005

Fitzhenry & Whiteside acknowledges with thanks the Canada Council for the Arts,
the Government of Canada through the Book Publishing Industry Development Program (BPIDP),
and the Ontario Arts Council for their support of our publishing program.

Cover and Book Design by Wycliffe Smith Design
Printed in Hong Kong.

Omar On Board

The end-of-school party was a great success. Everyone was promoted, the snacks were delicious, and Ms. Fudge gave each student the perfect present.

Elsie was thrilled with her balloons, which
looked like a big bouquet when they were
blown up. Omar loved the way his goggles
made the world pink.

The party got even better when Ms. Fudge blew
her whistle for the swim meet to begin. Holding their
presents tight, they all trotted down to the pond.

Elsie worried that her balloon bouquet would
blow away, so Ms. Fudge tied it to Elsie's wrist and
she was happy about that.

When Ms. Fudge called for floating, everyone turned belly-up in the pond. Thomas spit fountains. Bart balanced his ball just right. Elsie gazed at her balloons swaying gently in the breeze.

Omar sank.

But Omar was not disappointed for long.
Soon it was time for the backstroke. He took off
like a rocket. Omar kicked fast and stroked hard.
But he swung so wide that he crashed into Elsie
and popped one of her balloons.

"I'm sorry, Elsie," said Omar.

"That's okay, Omar," said Elsie.

"I think my bouquet will be safer tied to a branch."

"I can't seem to do anything right in the pond today," said Omar.

"I think you will be great on the high dive," said Elsie.

Elsie is right, thought Omar. The others can float and swim, but no one can jump higher than I can.

In his ice skates Omar could jump on the frozen pond all winter.

When his turn came, Omar scampered right to the top of the steps.

But when he
stood at the end
of the board, Omar
could not move.

"When I count to three, jump, Omar!"
called Ms. Fudge. "ONE…TWO…THREE!"
But Omar could not jump. "Four," said Ms. Fudge.
But still Omar could not jump.

"Don't worry, Omar," called Elsie. "It's easy!
You can do it!"

Omar *did* worry. He could *not* do it. His stomach
felt funny and his knees wobbled. He stood there,
high up and all alone. The wind rustled around him.
Everyone seemed so far away.

Finally Omar did the only thing he could do. He turned around, crouched down, and crawled back. Slowly he made his way down the steps.

The others jumped off the board so easily. But for Omar, it was impossible.

"Don't be sad, Omar," said Elsie. "In winter, you are the best on the pond."

"I don't care if I'm the best in winter," he said. "I just want to have fun in the pond today!"

Then Elsie noticed something terrible. Somehow her balloons had become untied, and they were drifting off in the breeze.

"Oh no!" cried Elsie.

Omar jumped up. "Don't worry, Elsie. I will get them!"

When the balloons floated
over a hill, Omar ran
over the hill.

When they floated low, he ran low.

When a gust of wind carried
the balloons higher, Omar
was just behind them.

He never let them out of his
sight. Not even once.

Now the balloons were right
in front of Omar.

He stretched out…and
stretched out…until
he grabbed the strings
and held them tight!

Omar floated down gently into the pond.

When Omar popped up, the whole class was cheering.

"It was easy," said Omar as he handed Elsie her balloons.

Elsie was so happy to have her bouquet back that she untied a balloon and offered it to Omar. "Take one," she said. "Balloons are lucky for you."

"I will never let it go," said Omar.

And he didn't.